MW00906425

Nursery Rhymes

First published in 2014 by Miles Kelly Publishing Ltd
Harding's Barn, Bardfield End Green, Thaxted, Essex, CM6 3PX, UK

This edition printed 2021

2 4 6 8 10 9 7 5 3 1

Publishing Director Belinda Gallagher
Creative Director Jo Cowan
Editorial Director Rosie Neave
Design Manager Joe Jones
Image Manager Liberty Newton
Production Elizabeth Collins, Jennifer Brunwin-Jones
Reprographics Stephan Davis
Assets Lorraine King

ISBN 978-1-78989-312-0

Printed in China

British Library Cataloguing-in-Publication Data
A catalogue record for this book is available from the British Library

ACKNOWLEDGEMENTS
The publishers would like to thank the following artists who have contributed to this book:
Singing Rhymes: The Pope Twins (Advocate Art)
Playing Rhymes: Hannah Wood (Advocate Art)
Number Rhymes: Sharon Harmer (The Bright Agency)
Bedtime Rhymes: Luciana Feito

Made with paper from a sustainable forest

www.mileskelly.net

Contents

Singing Rhymes

Little Bo-peep

Little Bo-peep has lost her sheep
And doesn't know where to find them.
Leave them alone and they'll come home,
Bringing their tails behind them.

Jack and Jill

Jack and Jill went up the hill
To fetch a pail of water.
Jack fell down and broke his crown
And Jill came tumbling after.

Up Jack got and home did trot
As fast as he could caper.
He went to bed to mend his head
With vinegar and brown paper.

Sing a Song of Sixpence

Sing a song of sixpence,
A pocket full of rye.
Four and twenty blackbirds,
Baked in a pie.

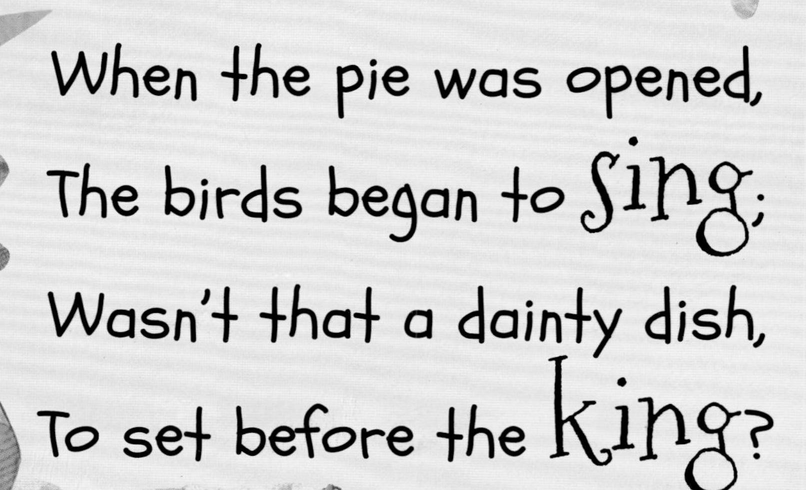

When the pie was opened,
The birds began to sing;
Wasn't that a dainty dish,
To set before the king?

The king was in his counting house,
Counting out his money;
The queen was in the parlour,
Eating bread and honey.

The maid was in the garden,
Hanging out the clothes;
When down came a blackbird
And pecked off her nose!

Three Blind Mice

Three blind mice,
three blind mice,
See how they run, see how they run!
They all ran after the farmer's wife,
Who cut off their tails with a carving knife,
Did you ever see such a thing in your life,
As three blind mice?

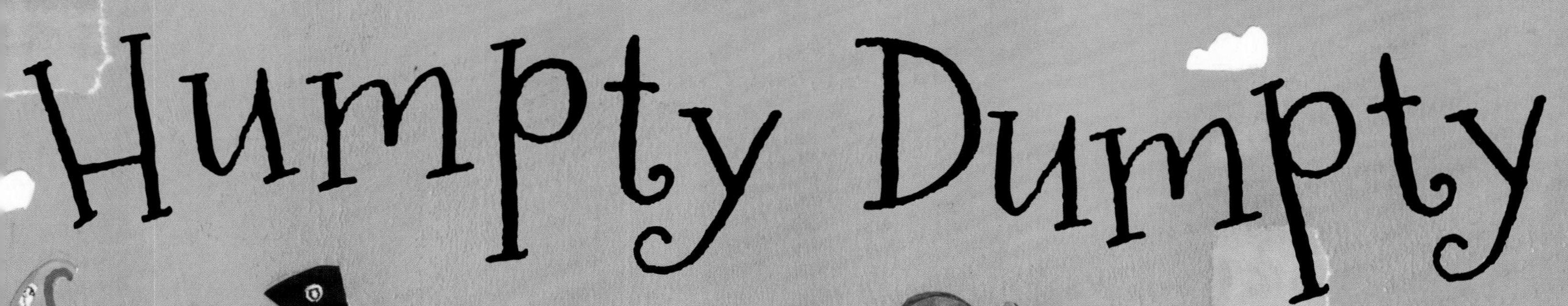

Humpty Dumpty

Humpty Dumpty sat on a wall,
Humpty Dumpty had a great fall
All the king's horses and all the king's men
Couldn't put Humpty together again.

Old Macdonald had a Farm

Old Macdonald had a farm, E-I-E-I-O!
And on that farm he had some cows, E-I-E-I-O!
With a moo-moo here,
And a moo-moo there,
Here a moo, there a moo,
Everywhere a moo-moo,
Old Macdonald had a farm, E-I-E-I-O!
moo-moo moo-moo

Old Macdonald had a farm, E-I-E-I-O!
And on that farm he had some sheep, E-I-E-I-O!
With a baa-baa here,
And a baa-baa there,
Here a baa, there a baa,
everywhere a baa-baa,
Old Macdonald had a farm, E-I-E-I-O!
baa-baa
baa-baa

Old Macdonald had a farm, E-I-E-I-O!
And on that farm he had some ducks, E-I-E-I-O!
With a quack-quack here,
And a quack-quack there,
Here a quack, there a quack,
everywhere a quack-quack,
Old Macdonald had a farm, E-I-E-I-O!

Old Macdonald had a farm, E-I-E-I-O!
And on that farm he had some pigs, E-I-E-I-O!
With an oink-oink here,
And an oink-oink there,
Here an oink, there an oink,
everywhere an oink-oink,
Old Macdonald had a farm, E-I-E-I-O!

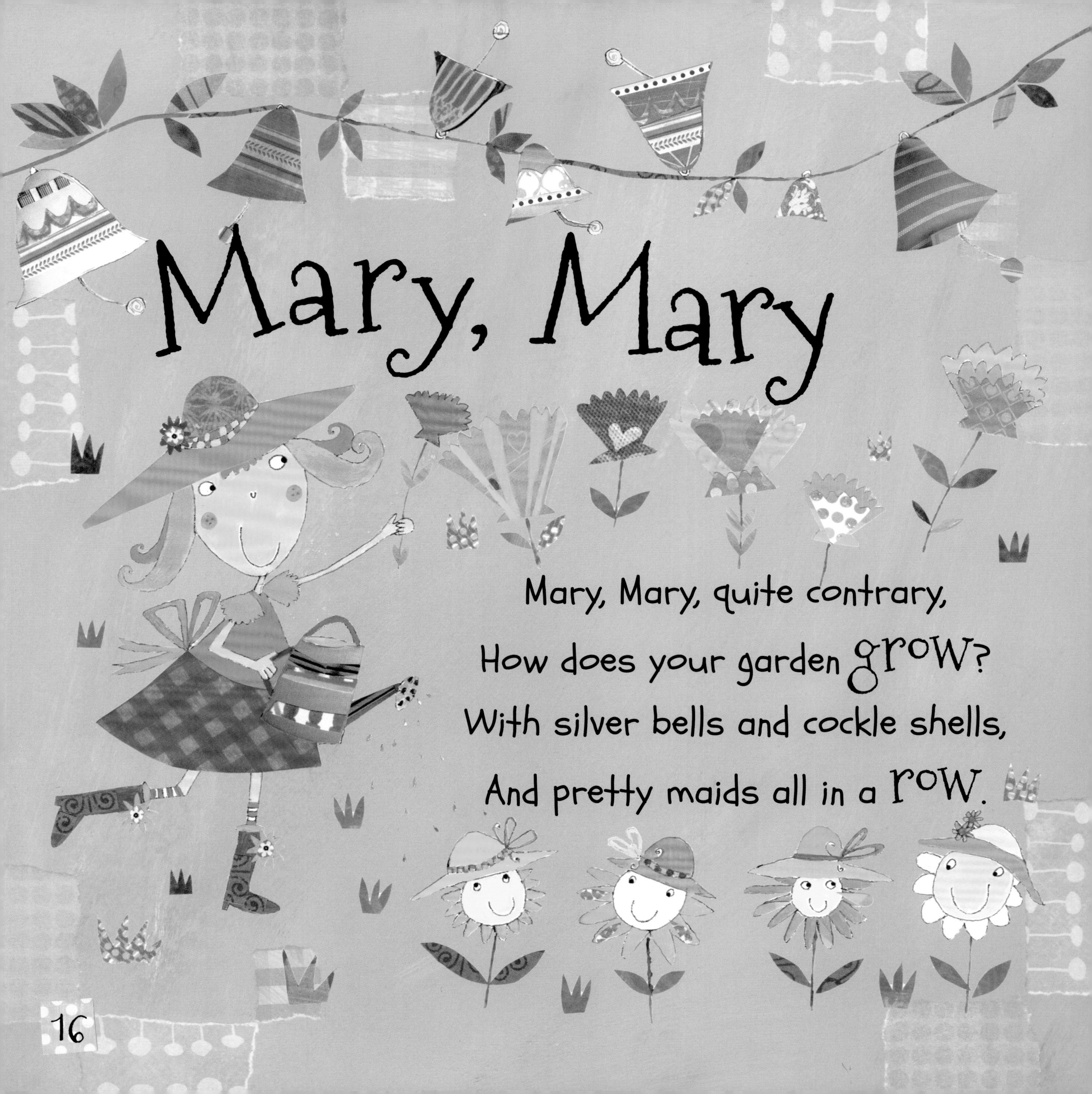

Mary, Mary

Mary, Mary, quite contrary,
How does your garden grow?
With silver bells and cockle shells,
And pretty maids all in a row.

Baa, Baa, Black Sheep

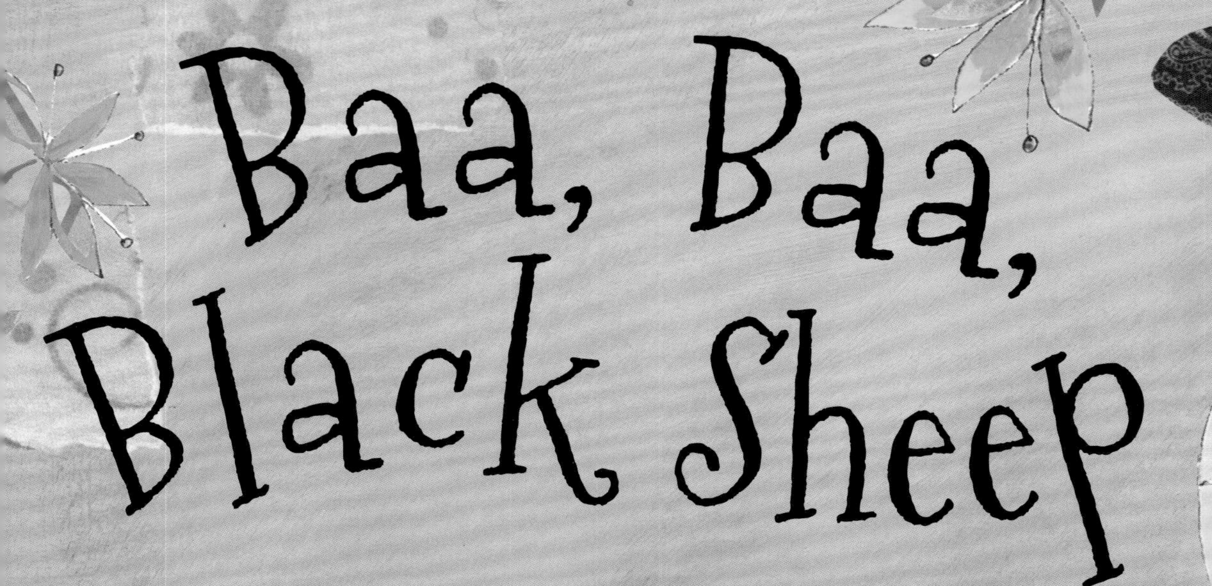

Baa, baa, black sheep,
Have you any wool?
Yes, sir, yes, sir,
Three bags full.
One for the master,
One for the dame,
And one for the little boy
Who lives down the lane.

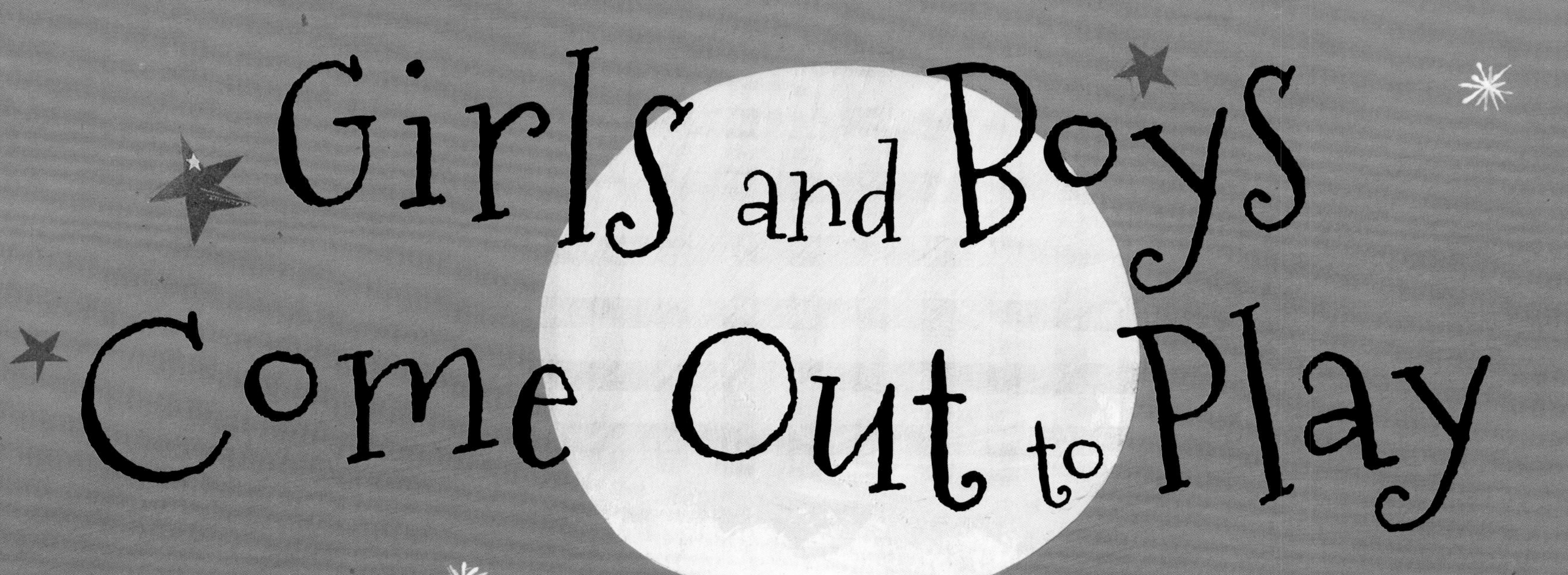

Girls and Boys Come Out to Play

Girls and boys come out to play,
The moon does shine as bright as day.
Leave your supper, and leave your sleep,
And come with your playfellows into the street.

Come with a whoop, come with a call,
Come with a good will or not at all.
Up the ladder and down the wall,
A halfpenny loaf will serve us all.
You find milk, and I'll find flour,
And we'll have a pudding in half an hour.

Polly Put the Kettle on

Polly put the kettle on,
Polly put the kettle on,
Polly put the kettle on,
And let's have tea.

Sukey take it off again,
Sukey take it off again,
Sukey take it off again,
They've all gone away.

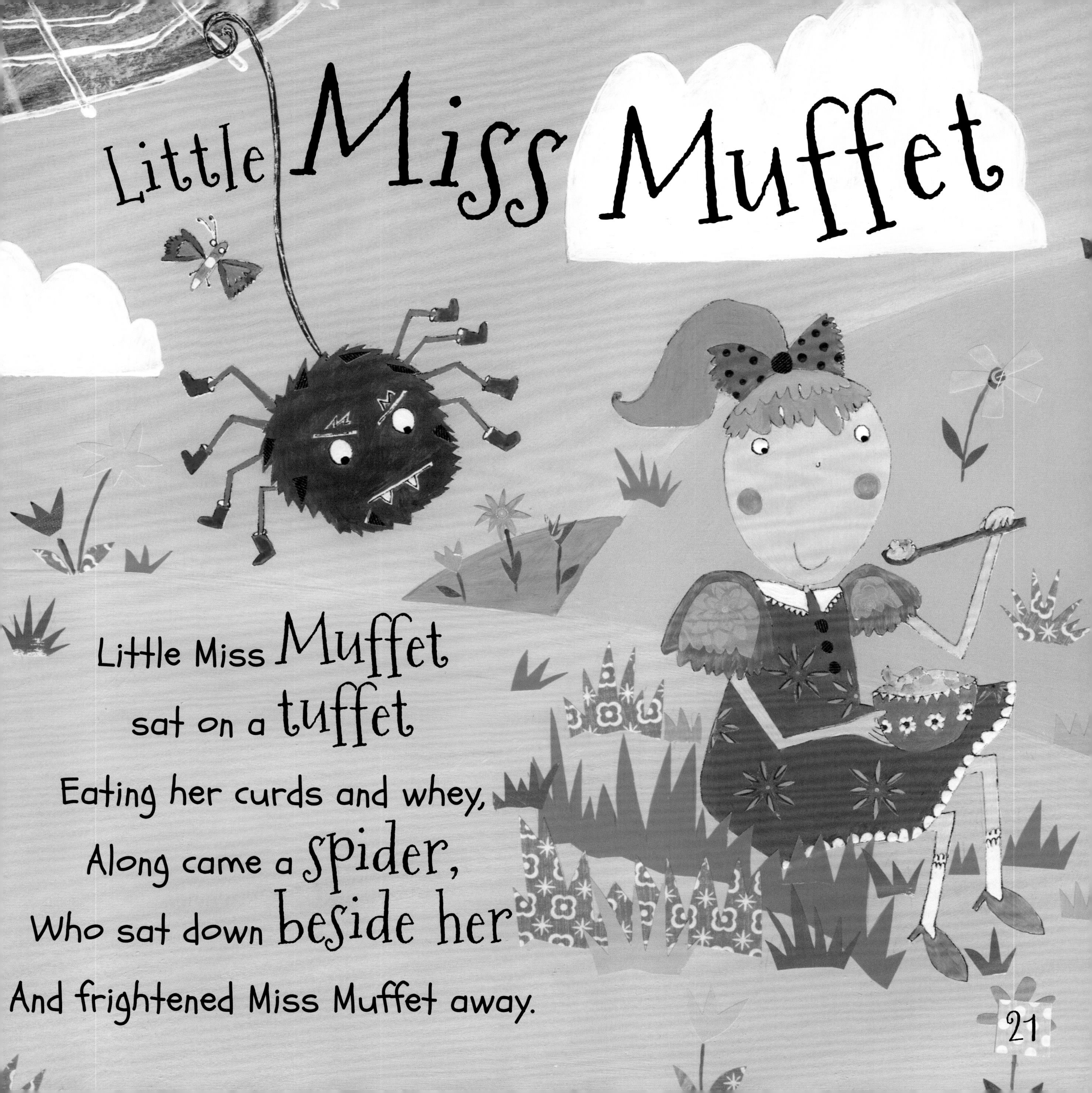

Little Miss Muffet

Little Miss Muffet
sat on a tuffet
Eating her curds and whey,
Along came a spider,
Who sat down beside her
And frightened Miss Muffet away.

The Wheels on the Bus

The wheels on the bus go
round and round,
Round and round,
round and round.
The wheels on the bus go
round and round,
All day long.

The horn on the bus goes
Beep, beep, beep,
Beep, beep, beep,
Beep, beep, beep.
The horn on the bus goes
Beep, beep, beep,
All day long.

The windscreen wipers go
Swish, swish, swish,
Swish, swish, swish,
Swish, swish, swish,
The windscreen wipers go
Swish, swish, swish,
All day long.

The people on the bus bounce

up and down,

Up and down, up and down.

The people on the bus bounce

up and down,

All day long.

The daddies on the bus go

nod, nod, nod,

Nod, nod, nod, nod, nod, nod.

The daddies on the bus go

nod, nod, nod,

All day long.

The mummies on the bus go
chatter, chatter, chatter,
Chatter, chatter, chatter,
chatter, chatter, chatter.
The mummies on the bus go
chatter, chatter, chatter,
All day long.

Pease Porridge Hot

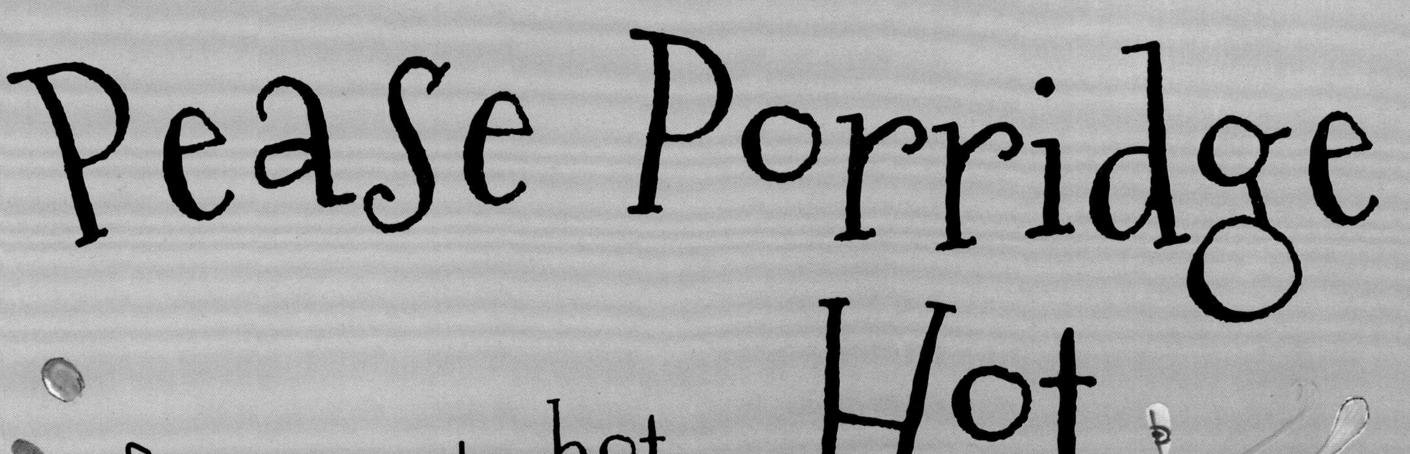

Pease porridge hot,
Pease porridge cold,
Pease porridge in the pot
Nine days old.

Some like it hot,
Some like it cold,
Some like it in the pot
Nine days old!

Hey Diddle Diddle

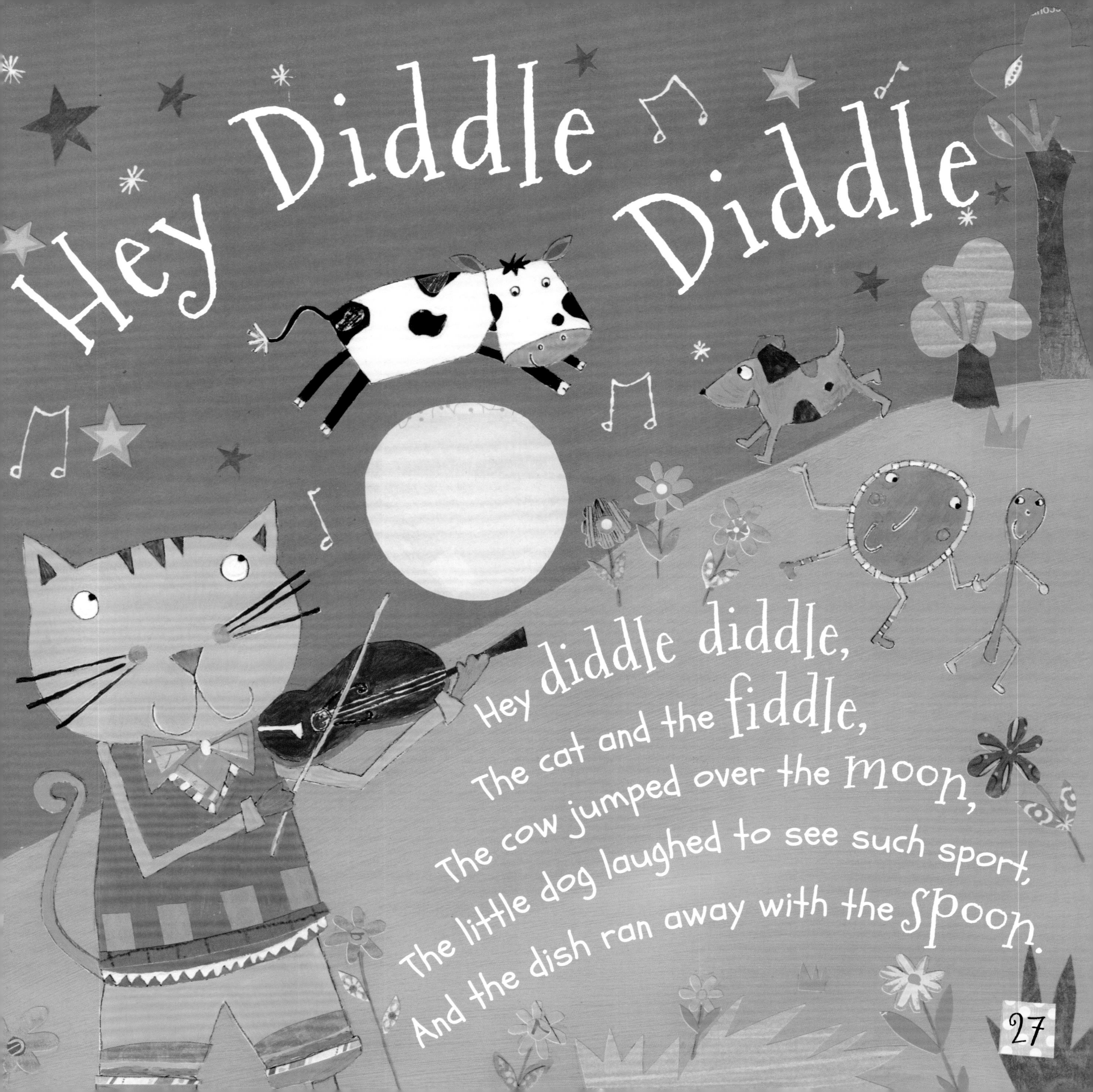

Hey diddle diddle,
The cat and the fiddle,
The cow jumped over the moon,
The little dog laughed to see such sport,
And the dish ran away with the spoon.

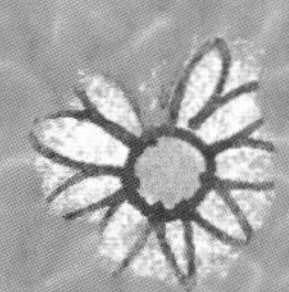

Playing Rhymes

Here is the Church

Link your fingers downwards with the back of your hands facing up to form the church. Point index fingers up to form the spire. Turn hands over and wiggle the fingers to be the people.

Here is the church, and here is the steeple,
Open the door and here are the people.
Here is the parson going upstairs,
And here he is a-saying his prayers.

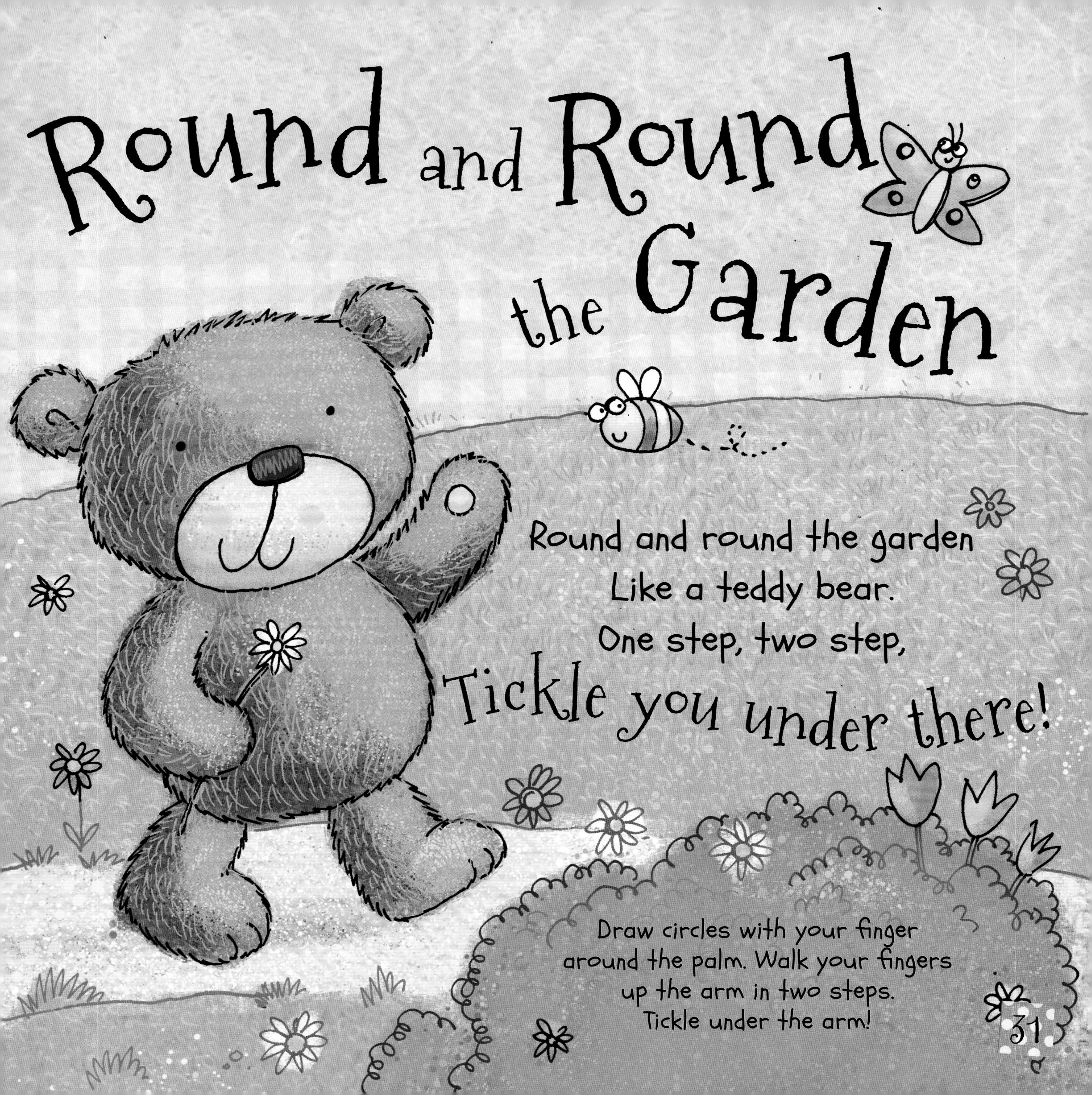
Round and Round the Garden
Round and round the garden
Like a teddy bear.
One step, two step,
Tickle you under there!
Draw circles with your finger
around the palm. Walk your fingers
up the arm in two steps.
Tickle under the arm!
31

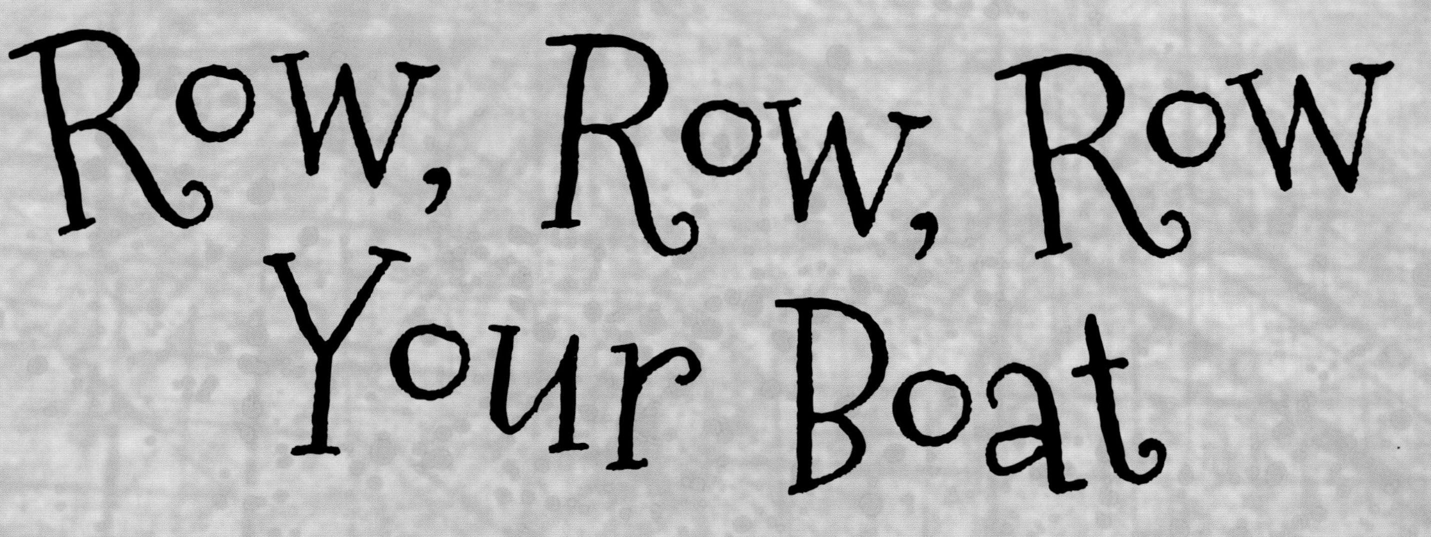

Row, Row, Row Your Boat

Row, row, row your boat
Gently down the stream.
Merrily, merrily, merrily, merrily,
Life is but a dream.

Sit across from your partner, holding hands and rocking back and forth. SCREAM on the second verse! ROAR on the third verse!

Row, row, row your boat
Gently down the stream.
If you see a crocodile,
Don't forget to SCREAM!

Row, row, row your boat
Gently to the shore.
If you see a lion,
Don't forget to ROAR!

This Little Pig

This little pig went to market,
This little pig stayed at home,
This little pig had roast beef,
This little pig had none,
And this little pig cried,
"Wee-Wee-Wee-Wee-Wee!"
All the way home.

Read the first line and wiggle the big toe.
Read the next line and wiggle the
next toe and so on. On the final line,
tickle the foot.
"Wee-Wee-Wee-Wee-Wee!"

Pat-a-Cake

Pat-a-cake, pat-a-cake, baker's man,
Bake me a cake as fast as you can.
Roll it and pat it and mark it with 'B',
And put it in the oven for
baby and me.

Clap your hands together then
pat the palms of your partner.
Repeat this action as you sing the rhyme.

I'm a Little Teapot

Place one hand on your hip to be the handle.
Place the other arm out to the side to be the spout.
On the final line, lean over to one side to pour the tea.

I'm a little teapot
Short and stout,
Here is my handle
Here is my spout.

When I see the teacups
Hear me shout,
"Tip me up and pour me out!"

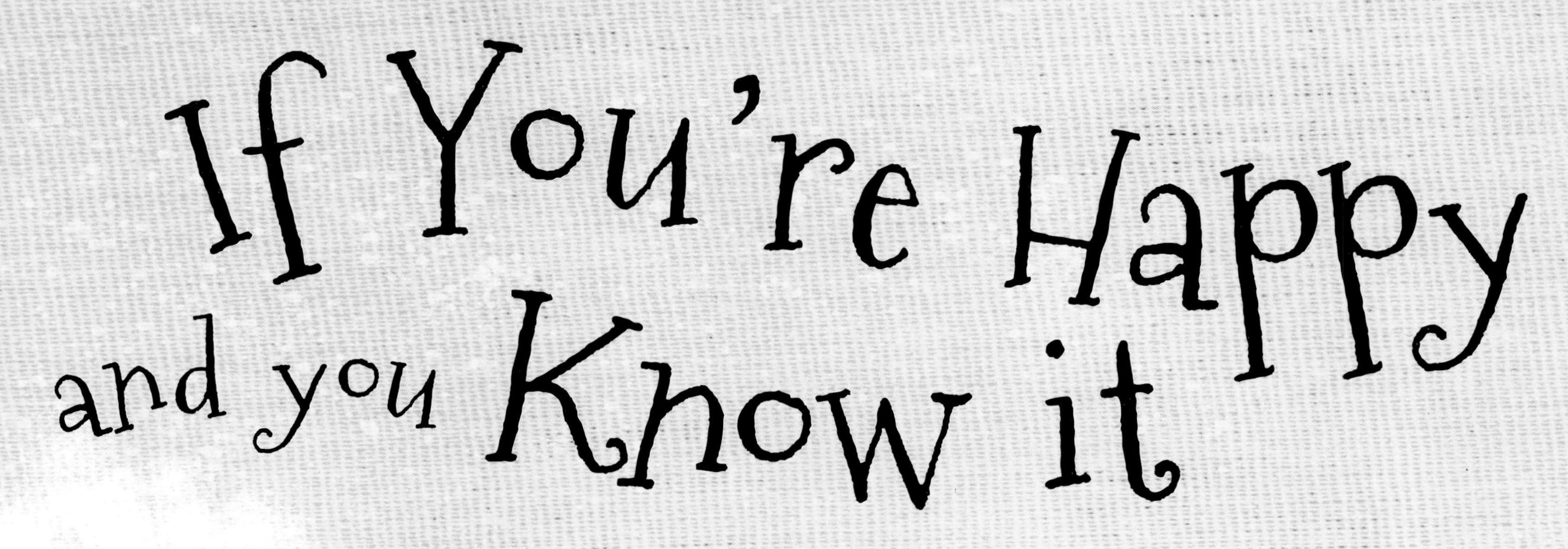

If You're Happy and you Know it

If you're happy and you know it,
Clap your hands!
If you're happy and you know it,
Clap your hands!

Repeat the words again, but change the action to stamping your feet, clicking your fingers and nodding your head.

If you're happy and you know it
And you really want to show it,
If you're happy and you know it

Clap your hands!

The Grand Old Duke of York

Oh, the grand old Duke of York,
He had ten thousand men,
He marched them up to the top of the hill
And he marched them down again.

March up and down on the
spot to get to the top of the hill.
March and crouch down to get down hill.
March half-crouching half-standing
to be neither up nor down.
And when they were up they were up,
And when they were down they were down,
And when they were only halfway up,
They were neither up nor down.

Head, Shoulders, Knees and Toes

Touch each part of the body as you sing the rhyme.

Head, shoulders, knees and toes,

Knees and toes.

Head, shoulders, knees and toes,

Knees and toes.

And eyes and ears and mouth and nose,

Head, shoulders, knees and toes,

Knees and toes.

Incy Wincy Spider

Incy Wincy Spider
Climbed up the water spout,
Down came the rain
And washed the spider out.

Use your fingers to be the spider climbing up the spout. Wiggle your fingers to be the rain. Sweep your hands in an arch to show the sun.

Out came the sun
And dried up all the rain,
So Incy Wincy Spider
Climbed up the spout again!

See-Saw, Margery Daw

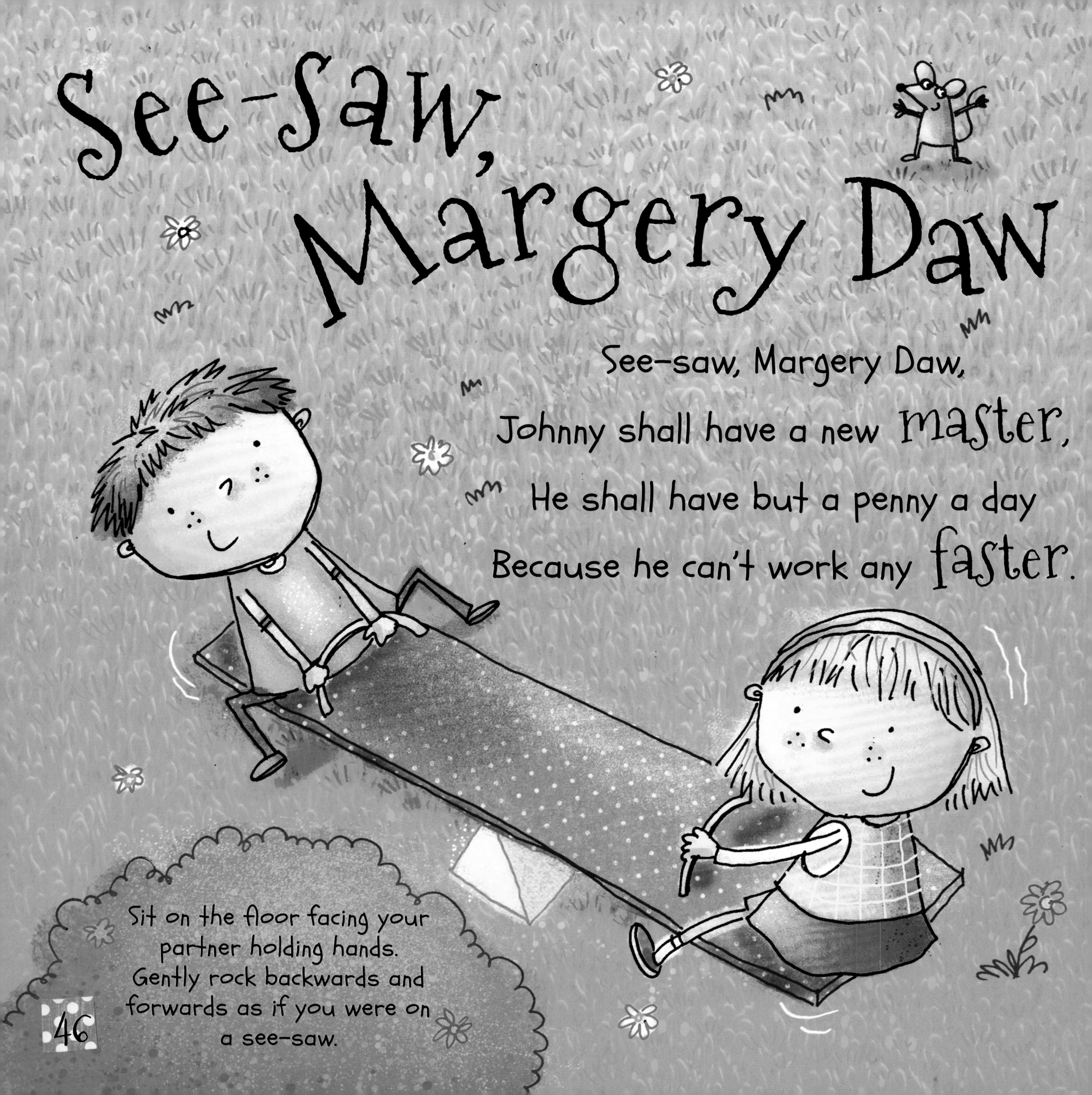

See-saw, Margery Daw,
Johnny shall have a new master,
He shall have but a penny a day
Because he can't work any faster.

Sit on the floor facing your partner holding hands. Gently rock backwards and forwards as if you were on a see-saw.

I Hear Thunder

I hear thunder, I hear thunder,
Hark, don't you, hark, don't you?
Pitter patter raindrops,
Pitter patter raindrops,
I'm wet through,
So are you.

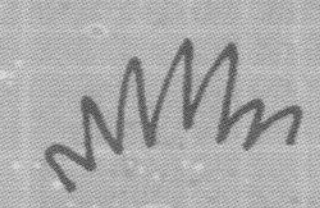

Stamp your feet on the ground to make thunder.
Wiggle your fingers to make raindrops.
Point to yourself. Point to your partner.

Ring-a-ring o' Roses

Ring-a-ring o' roses,
A pocket full of posies,
A-tishoo! A-tishoo!
We all fall down.

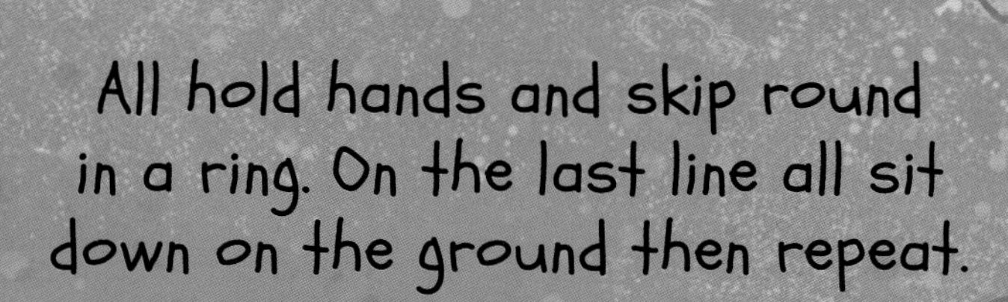

All hold hands and skip round in a ring. On the last line all sit down on the ground then repeat.

The king has sent his daughter
To fetch a pail of water,
A-tishoo! A-tishoo!
We all fall down.

The bird upon the steeple
Sits high above the people,
A-tishoo! A-tishoo!
We all fall down.

Rain

Rain on the green grass,
Rain on the trees,
Rain on the rooftop,
But not on me!

Make rain motions with your fingers.
Sweep hands around to form a treetop.
Form a roof over your head with
your hands. Point to yourself
with your index finger.

Number Rhymes

One Potato

One potato, two potato,
Three potato, four;
Five potato, six potato,
Seven potato more.

Hickety Pickety

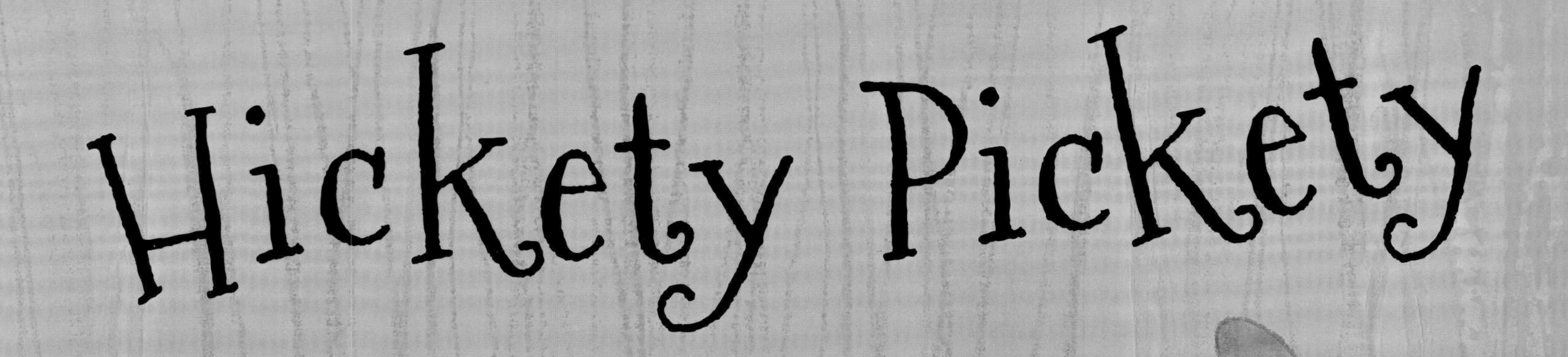

Hickety pickety my black hen,
She lays eggs for gentlemen.
Sometimes nine and
sometimes ten,
Hickety pickety my black hen.

Hickory Dickory Dock

Hickory dickory dock,
The mouse ran up the clock,
The clock struck one,
The mouse ran down,
Hickory, dickory, dock.

Hickory dickory dock,
The mouse ran up the clock,
The clock struck two,
The mouse said, "Boo!"
Hickory dickory dock.

Hickory dickory dock,
The mouse ran up the clock,
The clock struck three,
The mouse said, "Weeee!"
Hickory dickory dock.

Hickory dickory dock,
The mouse ran up the clock,
The clock struck four,
Let's sing some more,
Hickory dickory dock.

Five Little Ducks

Five little ducks went
swimming one day,
Over the hill and far away.
Mother duck said, "Quack,
quack, quack, quack!"
And only four little ducks
came back.

Four little ducks went
swimming one day,
Over the hill and far away.
Mother duck said, "Quack,
quack, quack, quack!"
And only three little ducks
came back.

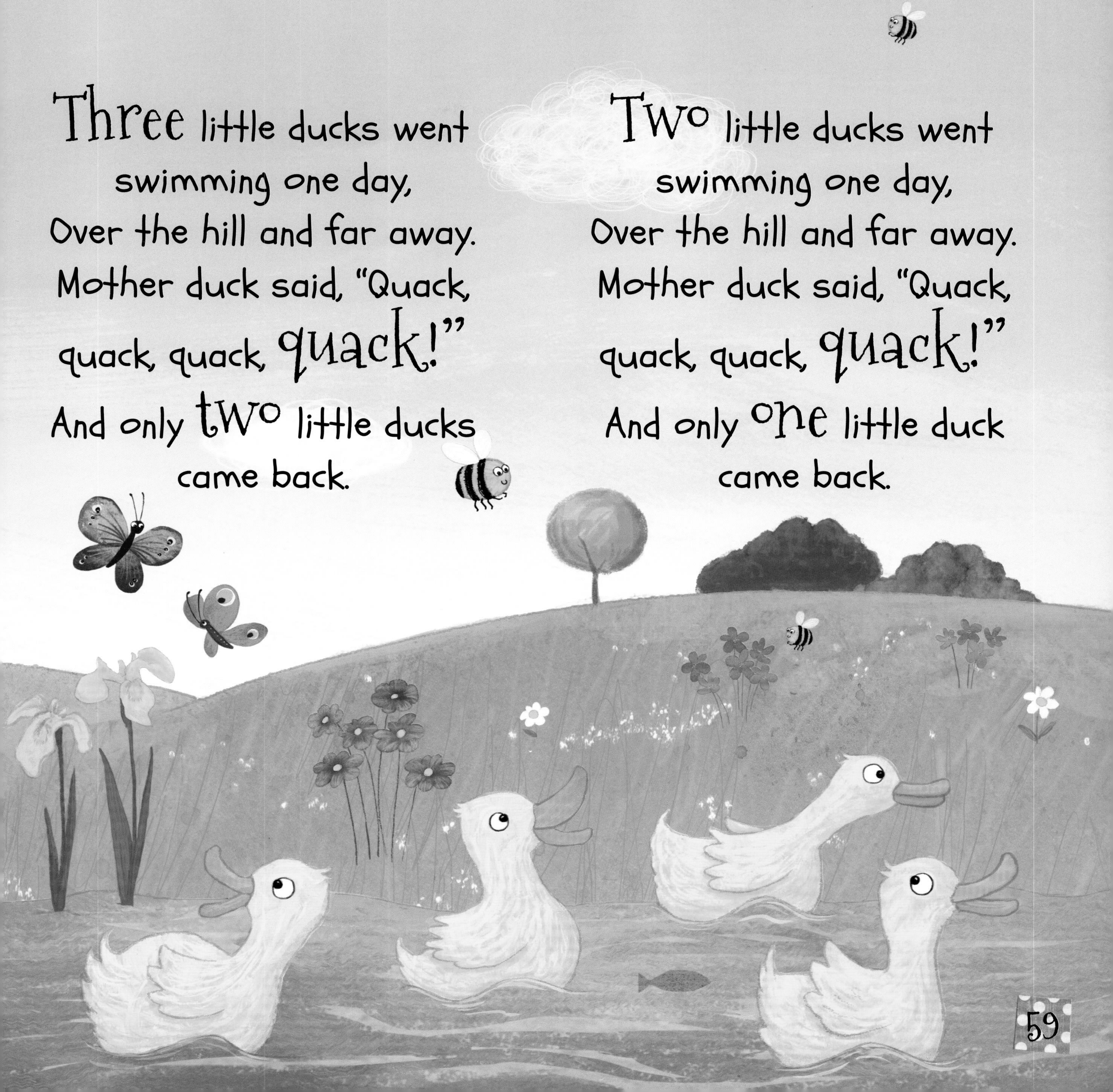

Three little ducks went
swimming one day,
Over the hill and far away.
Mother duck said, "Quack,
quack, quack, quack!"
And only two little ducks
came back.

Two little ducks went
swimming one day,
Over the hill and far away.
Mother duck said, "Quack,
quack, quack, quack!"
And only one little duck
came back.

One little duck went
swimming one day,
Over the hill and far away.
Mother duck said,
"Quack, quack,
quack, quack!"
And all her five little ducks
came back.

Rub-a-dub-dub

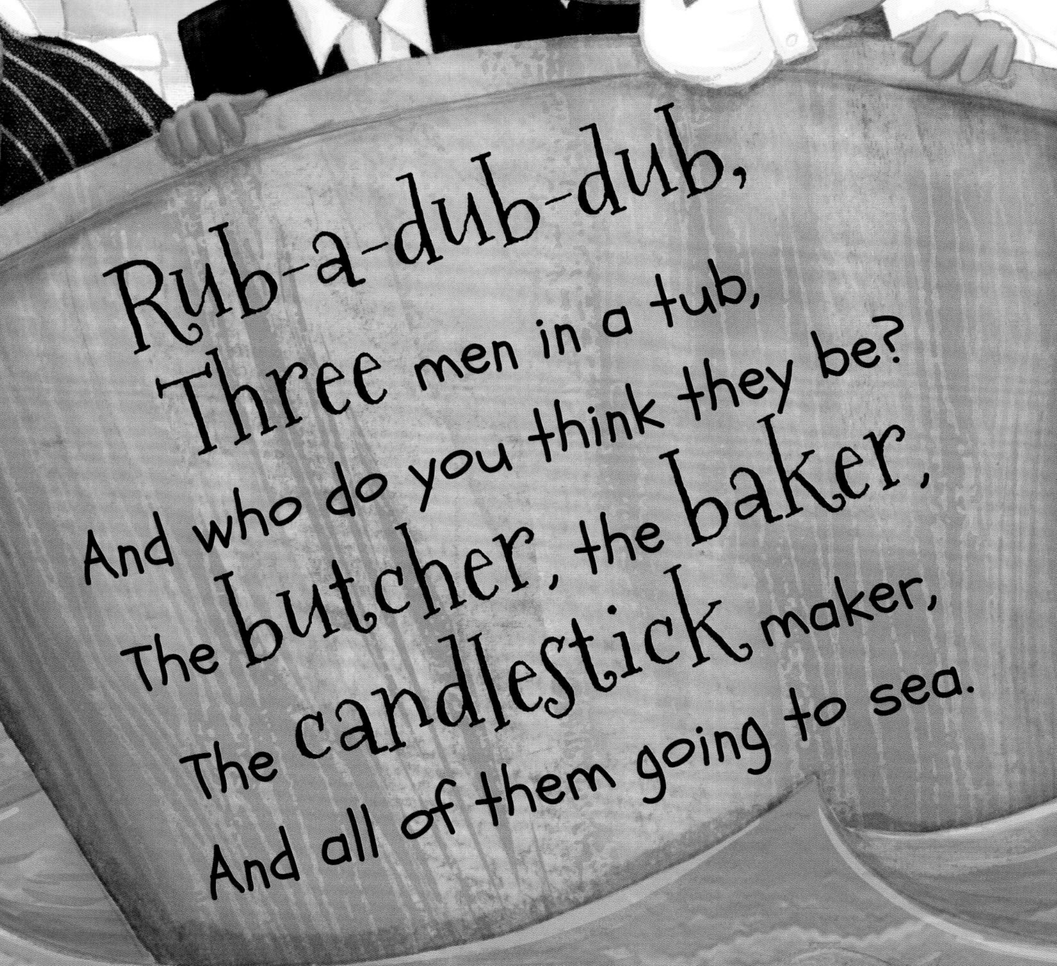

Rub-a-dub-dub,
Three men in a tub,
And who do you think they be?
The butcher, the baker,
The candlestick maker,
And all of them going to sea.

One, Two, Three, Four, Five

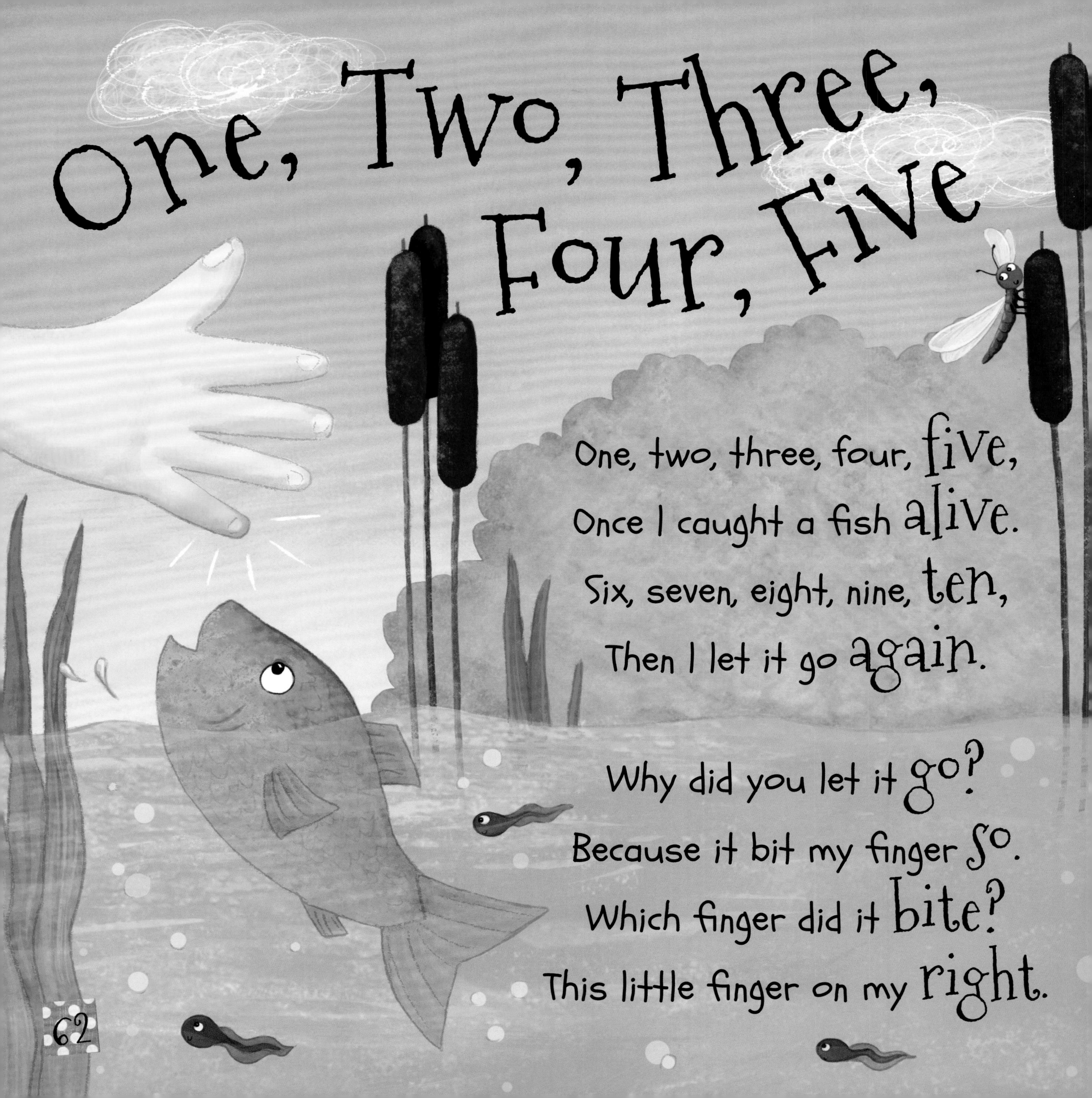

One, two, three, four, five,
Once I caught a fish alive.
Six, seven, eight, nine, ten,
Then I let it go again.

Why did you let it go?
Because it bit my finger so.
Which finger did it bite?
This little finger on my right.

Two Little Dicky Birds

Two little dicky birds sitting on a wall,
One named Peter, one named Paul.
Fly away Peter, fly away Paul,
Come back Peter, come back Paul!

One, Two, Buckle my Shoe

One, two,
buckle my shoe.

Three, four,
knock at the door.

Five, six, pick up sticks.

Seven, eight, lay them straight.

Nine, ten,
a good fat hen.

Five Little Pussy-cats

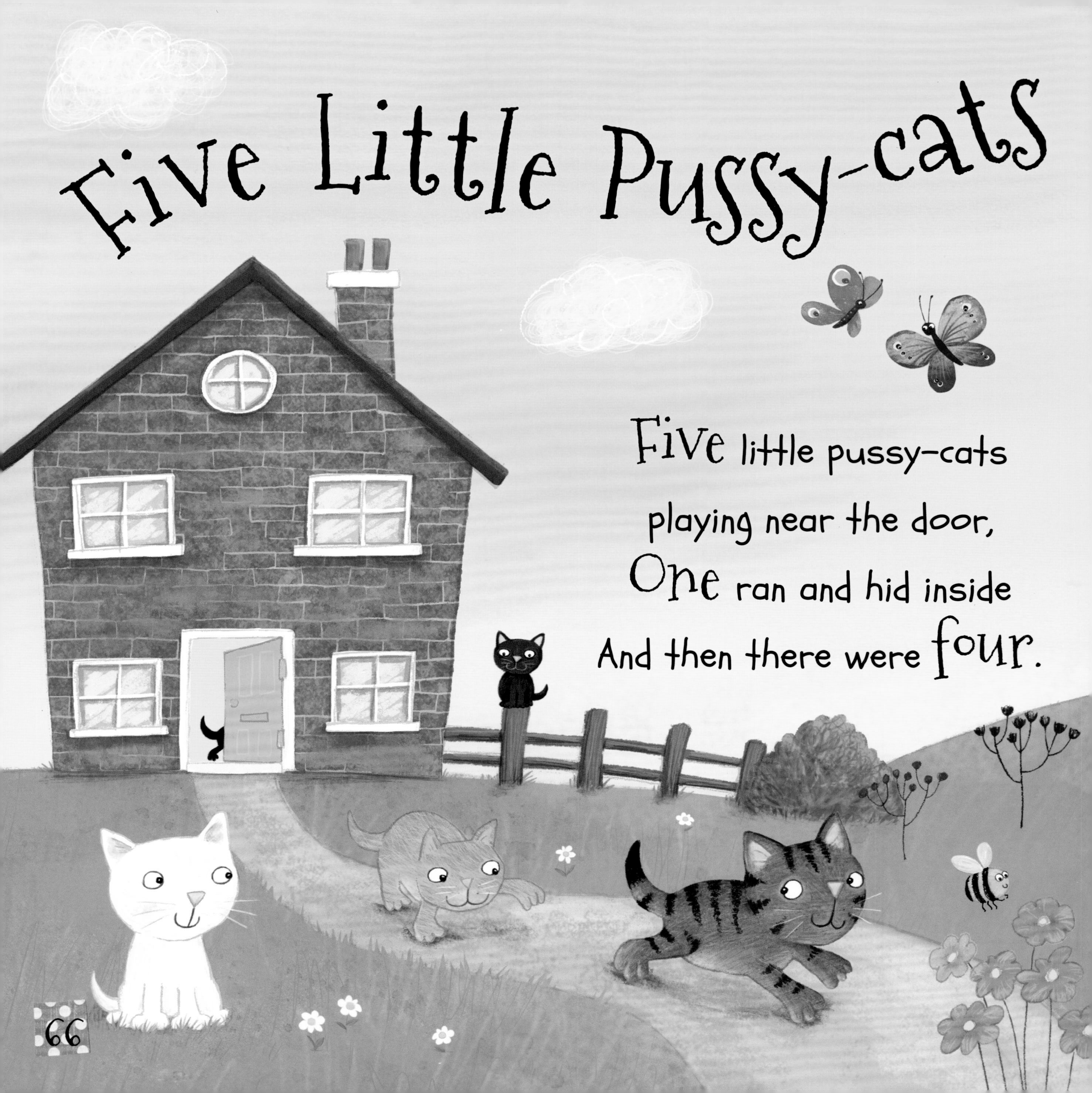

Five little pussy-cats
playing near the door,
One ran and hid inside
And then there were four.

Four little pussy-cats
underneath a tree,
One heard a dog bark
And then there were three.

Three little pussy-cats
thinking what to do,
One saw a little bird
And then there were two.

Two little pussy-cats
sitting in the sun,
One ran to catch his tail
And then there was one.

One little pussy-cat looking
for some fun,
He saw a butterfly
And then there were none.

One, Two, Three, Four

One, two, three, four,
Mary at the kitchen door.
Five, six, seven, eight,
Eating cherries off a plate.

Hot Cross Buns!

Hot cross buns! Hot cross buns!
One a penny, two a penny,
Hot cross buns!
Give them to your daughters,
Give them to your sons,
One a penny, two a penny,
Hot cross buns!

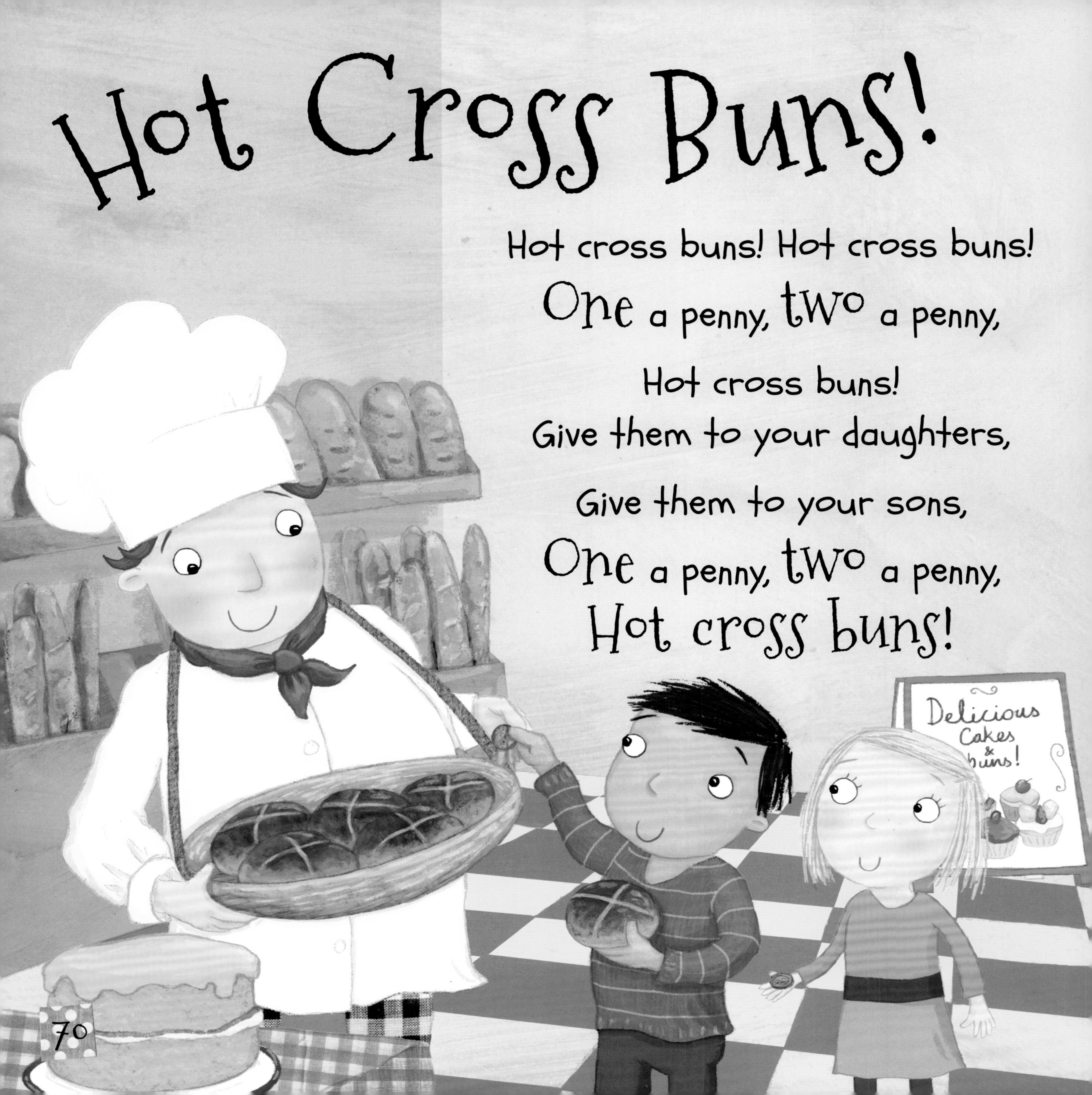

Five Little Peas

Five little peas
In a peapod pressed,
One grew, two grew,
And so did all the rest.
They grew and grew
And did not stop,
Until one day
The peapod popped!

I Saw Three Ships

I saw three ships
come sailing by,
Come sailing by,
Come sailing by,
I saw three ships
come sailing by,
On New Year's Day
in the morning.

And what do you think was in them then,
Was in them then, was in them then?
And what do you think was in them then,

On New Year's Day in the morning?

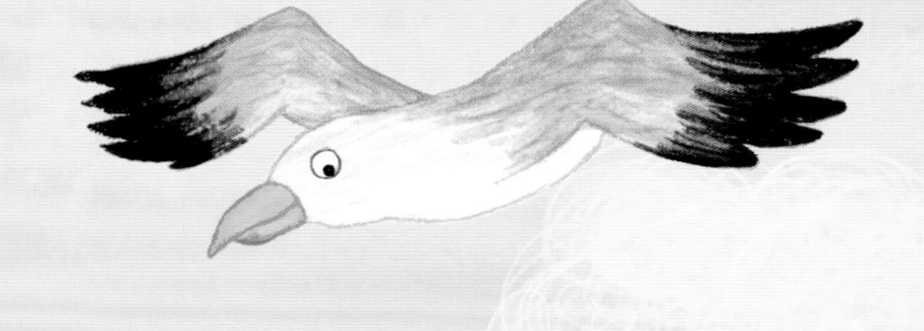

Three pretty girls
were in them then,
Were in them then,
were in them then,
Three pretty girls
were in them then,
On New Year's Day in the morning.

One for Sorrow

One for sorrow,
Two for joy,
Three for a girl,
Four for a boy.
Five for silver,

Six for gold,
Seven for a secret,
Never to be told.
Eight for a wish,
Nine for a kiss,
Ten for a bird you want to miss.

Bedtime Rhymes

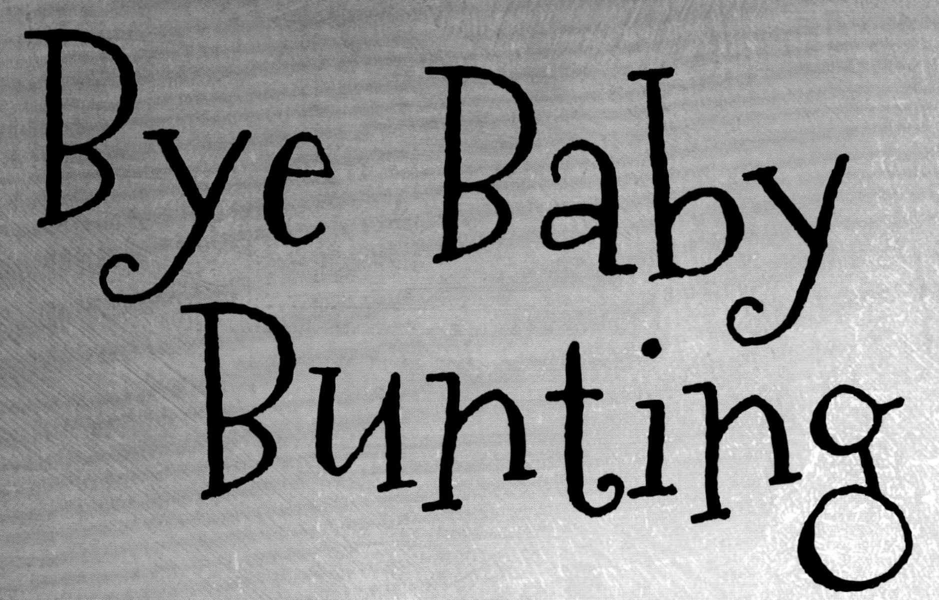

Bye Baby Bunting

Bye baby bunting,
Daddy's gone a-hunting,
To get a little rabbit-skin,
To wrap his little baby in.

I See the Moon

I see the moon,
And the moon sees me.
God bless the moon,
And God bless me!

Rock-a-Bye Baby

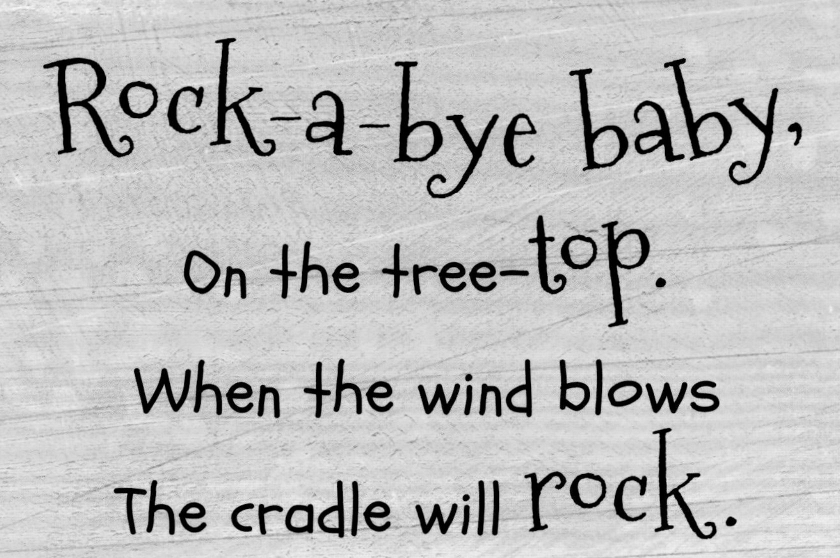

Rock-a-bye baby,
On the tree-top.
When the wind blows
The cradle will rock.

When the bough breaks
The cradle will fall.
Down will come baby,
Cradle and all.

Twinkle, Twinkle, Little Star

Twinkle, twinkle, little star,
How I wonder what you are.
Up above the world so high,
Like a diamond in the sky.

When the blazing sun is gone,
When he nothing shines upon,
Then you show your little light,
Twinkle, twinkle, all the night.

Hush Little Baby

Hush, little baby, don't say a word,
Papa's going to buy you a mocking bird.
If that mocking bird won't sing,
Papa's going to buy you a diamond ring.
If that diamond ring turns to brass,
Papa's going to buy you a looking-glass.

If that looking-glass gets broke,
Papa's going to buy you a billy-goat.
If that billy-goat runs away,
Papa's going to buy you another today.

Wee Willie Winkie

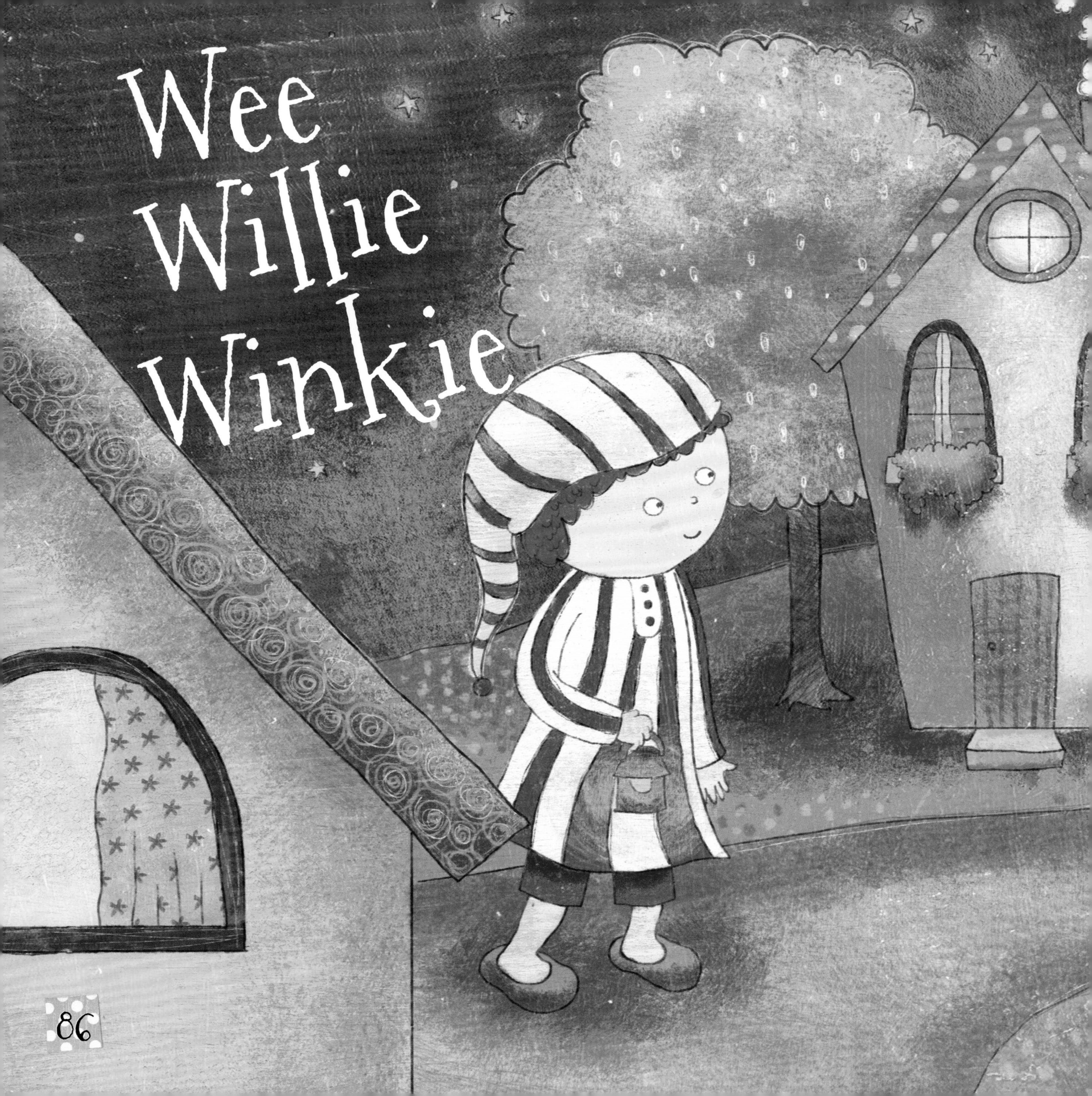

Wee Willie Winkie
Runs through the town,
Upstairs and downstairs
In his nightgown.
Rapping at the window,
Crying through the lock,
"Are the children in their beds,
For now it's eight o'clock?"

Teddy Bear, Teddy Bear

Teddy bear, teddy bear, touch the ground.
Teddy bear, teddy bear, turn around.
Teddy bear, teddy bear, show your shoe.
Teddy bear, teddy bear, that will do.

Teddy bear, teddy bear, run upstairs.
Teddy bear, teddy bear, say your prayers.
Teddy bear, teddy bear, blow out the light.

Teddy bear, teddy bear,
say GOODNIGHT.

A Candle, a Candle

A candle, a candle to light me to bed,
A pillow, a pillow to tuck up my head.
The moon is as sleepy as sleepy can be,
The stars are all pointing their fingers at me.

And Missus Hop-Robin, way up in her nest,
Is rocking her tired little babies to rest.
So give me a blanket to tuck up my toes,
And a little soft pillow to snuggle my nose.

Diddle Diddle Dumpling

Diddle diddle dumpling,
My son John,
Went to bed
With his trousers on.
One shoe off,
And one shoe on,

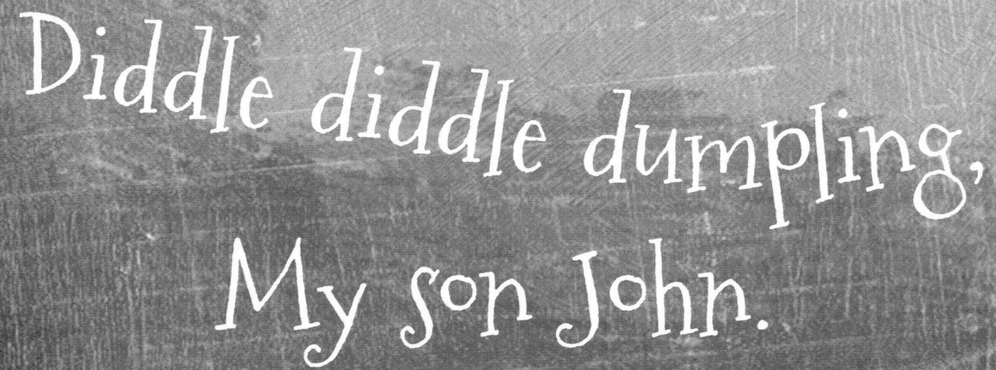

Diddle diddle dumpling,
My son John.

Star Light, Star Bright

Star light, star bright,
First star I see tonight.
I wish I may, I wish I might,
Have the wish I wish tonight.

The Evening is Coming

The evening is coming,
The sun sinks to rest,
The birds are all flying
Straight home to the nest.

"Caw," says the crow
As he flies overhead,
"It's time little children
Were going to bed!"

The Man in the Moon

The man in the moon
Looked out of the moon,
And this is what he said,
"'Tis time that now I'm getting up,
All babies went to bed."